DRACULA

~

The Essex Connection!

Ian Yearsley

Published by Ian Yearsley

Publishing partner: Paragon Publishing, Rothersthorpe
First published 2018
© Ian Yearsley 2018

ISBN 978-1-78222-578-2

Book design, layout and production management by Into Print
www.intoprint.net
+44 (0)1604 832149

CONTENTS

AUTHOR'S NOTE

At the beginning of 1990 I read a book by David Weaver called *Essex Tales*. It comprised several short, illustrated articles about aspects of Essex. One of the articles covered the topic of "Purfleet Vampires". It stated that Bram Stoker, author of *Dracula*, the classic gothic, horror novel that spawned a whole vampire industry, had his principal character, Count Dracula, base his operations in the south-west Essex village of Purfleet. This, at the time, was news to me.

The copy of "Essex Tales" which, in 1990, set the author off on a Dracula goose-chase!

The article concluded as follows:

"It seems that Stoker had only a nodding acquaintance with the place and chose Purfleet as a foggy, out-of-the-way Thameside village, where no-one ever went. Unless, of course, you know different!"

I was 25 at the time and I saw that last phrase as a challenge! I consequently set out – almost immediately – to find out if there was any Essex fact behind Bram Stoker's fiction.

My starting point was to read Bram Stoker's *Dracula*, originally published in 1897. It became, and still is, one of my favourite books.

I then spent much of that spring and the first part of the summer either in Purfleet, speaking to local people and viewing locations, or at the Essex Record Office, researching the Purfleet of Stoker's time. My primary objective was to try to match the people and places in *Dracula* with the people and places of late-19th-century Purfleet.

I soon found out that there was indeed some fact behind the fiction and I wrote up my findings into a manuscript and put it in my drawer. It stayed there until 1992, when I revisited it on the release of the film, "Bram Stoker's Dracula", starring Gary Oldman. I wrote an article summarising my findings for the April 1992 edition of "Essex Countryside" magazine (pp. 15-16). This reignited my interest in the topic and I updated my manuscript in 1994.

I revisited it again in 1997 on the centenary of the publication of Stoker's novel and I sent a copy of my manuscript to Thurrock historian, Jonathan Catton, who was carrying out similar research that year for Thurrock Museum in Grays. I believe that Jonathan would have like to have helped me get it published, but the museum did not have the funding available at the time. I also donated a copy of the manuscript and, in 2008, my research papers, to the Essex Record Office (under references T/Z 490/2 and T2559).

And that was how I left it until the end of 2017 when I got my manuscript out again, re-read it afresh and thought that it deserved a wider audience. I revisited my old haunts in Purfleet in February 2018 and I discovered that some things had changed, and some remained the same. Awareness of the Dracula connection in the village certainly seems greater now than it was in 1990, not least because of Jonathan's hard work in promoting the connection locally. There is now a plaque on the wall of St Stephen's church commemorating Dracula, which was not there 28 years ago. The Purfleet Heritage & Military Centre, which was opened in 1995, also contains a section on the

Dracula connection; the consultation material available for this includes a copy of my 1992 "Essex Countryside" article.

The commemorative plaque on the wall of St Stephen's Church

What follows is essentially what I wrote in 1990. I have updated it to reflect geographical changes that have taken place in Purfleet since that time, but the main text is largely how I wrote it then; my findings are, after all, as valid now as they were in 1990 and I consider the research that I carried out then to be an important contribution both to Essex local history and to vampire literature.

I hope this book is of interest to local people and Dracula fans alike. My wish is that it helps share the growing amount of knowledge and information about the connection between a small Essex village and one of the great landmark books of English gothic literature.

Ian Yearsley, Eastwood, Essex
11 February 2018

PREFACE

The story of Count Dracula, the blood-sucking vampire of Bram Stoker's classic gothic horror novel and the subsequent star of a multitude of stage and film presentations, is well-known: a creature which comes alive at night when everyone else is asleep to feast on the warm blood of young maidens before returning to its coffin home at dawn; one which can be repelled by garlic and crosses but killed only by a stake through the heart. What is not so well known is that much of Stoker's original 1897 novel is set in Essex – in the Thameside village (as it was then) of Purfleet, near Grays.

Why should Bram Stoker have chosen such a seemingly insignificant settlement as the place where the Transylvanian vampire makes his English home? Could it be that the fiction of *Dracula* is based on some horrifying fact? Does Purfleet perhaps have a history of vampire associations? Are the characters and the locations in the novel drawn from actual people and places in the village? Or is there a more mundane reason for this Essex location being Stoker's choice?

This book sets out to answer all these questions and more to provide once and for all an answer to the mystery of why Bram Stoker should wish to set such a horrific blood-curdling story in a quiet Essex Thameside village...

I

BACKGROUND – BRAM STOKER AND "DRACULA"

Before an analysis of Purfleet's vampire associations is attempted, it will be helpful to those unfamiliar with Stoker and his work to look briefly at the life of this remarkable Victorian author and his connections with Purfleet and to give some account of *Dracula* in order first to set the scene which was to form the basis for these investigations.

Abraham ('Bram') Stoker was born in Clontarf, Dublin on 8th November 1847, the son of a civil servant who worked in Dublin Castle. He was the third oldest of seven children, but for the first seven years of his life, the young Bram was very ill and was confined to his bed for long periods as he was often unable even to walk.

Whilst he was lying in bed day-in, day-out, his mother, Charlotte, told him ghost stories, Irish folk stories and grisly tales of the recent cholera epidemics which had claimed hundreds of lives in Ireland and elsewhere. These included stories of people who were so ill with the disease that they were almost buried alive because they looked as if they were dead. Such stories were to stick in

Stoker's imagination and would become useful ingredients in later horror stories.

Despite his early illness, Stoker's health soon improved, and he was fit enough and well enough to qualify in his teens for a place at Trinity College at Dublin University, where he excelled at sport and took a keen interest in literature and the theatre, particularly in the work of the controversial American poet, Walt Whitman, and the performances of the up-and-coming actor, Henry Irving.

After University, Stoker was encouraged by his father to take a secure job in the Irish Civil Service and followed in his footsteps by working in Dublin Castle. Whilst there, he wrote his first widely-read book, a manual on *The Duties of Clerks of Petty Sessions in Ireland*, which was published in the late 1870s.

But Stoker was too interested in literature and theatre to be happy as a civil servant and he soon talked his way into an unpaid, part-time post as drama critic with the *Dublin Mail*. This liaison with the newspaper began when Stoker saw Irving in a play called *Two Roses*, a performance which was not reported in the press, but which Stoker himself had been to see three times in two weeks.

As well as his work on the newspaper, Stoker supplemented his civil service income by selling short horror stories, such as *The*

Chain of Destiny, which was published in the magazine *Shamrock* in 1875.

The following year Irving returned to Dublin to play the lead role in *Hamlet* and Stoker wrote in the *Mail* with such praise for his performance that he was invited back-stage to meet the actor. The two immediately became friends, a liaison which was ultimately to prove the most important in Stoker's career.

Stoker also managed to liaise at this time with Walt Whitman, to whom he had written several times before finally getting an answer and whom he was subsequently to meet twice when in the United States in later years.

Having met Irving in 1876, Stoker travelled to London in each of the following two years to see the actor at the Lyceum Theatre. Their friendship developed so well that in 1878, when Irving took over the running of the theatre himself, he invited Stoker to work for him there as theatre manager.

For one so interested in literature and theatre, Stoker did not need asking a second time. He resigned his job as a civil servant, married his long-time sweetheart, Florence Balcombe (once romantically linked with another Irish writer, Oscar Wilde), and moved to London. He was to stay there for the rest of his life.

Stoker ultimately became a very dependable

aid to Irving, running the theatre, organising theatre tours abroad and yet still managing his time well enough to be able to fit in some writing. He also mixed with other leading society figures of the day, including Wilde, the poet Alfred, Lord Tennyson, and the painter, James McNeill Whistler, and occupied a property at 27 Cheyne Walk, a sought-after London residential location.

Stories published by Stoker at this time included a collection of horror stories, entitled *Under the Sunset* (1881). He also became acquainted with the writer Thomas Hall Caine, who shared Stoker's interest in horror and the occult. Stoker was by now so immersed in the horror genre that he even mixed with members of the Golden Dawn Society (it's full title was "The Hermetic Order of the Golden Dawn"), a well-known organisation whose interests included magic, the occult and astrology. He may even have been a member himself.

His on-going interest in horror led him to research a great deal of related material and in 1891 his first major novel, *The Snake's Pass*, was well-received by the critics. It was not, however, to be until 1897 that Stoker finally made a breakthrough in his literary career, for this was the year that *Dracula* was published.

The effect of *Dracula* around the world has been astounding. Stoker drew on numerous contemporary and historical sources for information about vampires and no doubt reflected on some of the horror stories his mother had told him when he had been a child confined to his sick-bed. The story was an immediate success and, in the following century, was to become the subject of numerous stage and film presentations.

For those unfamiliar with the plot of *Dracula*, a brief resumé of it is given here, as it will be important to know, at the very least, the outline of the tale when considering its associations with the Essex village of Purfleet.

As the novel begins, the reader learns that Count Dracula, owner and sole inhabitant of a vast ruined castle, perched high on a lofty peak in the Carpathian Mountains of Transylvania (in modern-day Romania), has been negotiating with a firm of Exeter solicitors to purchase a property in England, close to the city of London. Jonathan Harker, the estate agents' representative, travels to Transylvania to provide the Count with details of an estate at Purfleet, in Essex, just a few miles to the east of the capital, which he has personally selected, and which, unbeknown to him and the reader, Dracula intends to use as a base for the furtherance of his evil vampire empire.

Having moved to England, landing at Whitby in Yorkshire hidden in a consignment of coffin-like wooden boxes which contain "hallowed" (i.e. sacred) earth, a kind of haven for vampires, the Count travels to Essex and takes residence in the property at Purfleet, from where he plans to thrive on the blood of his human victims during a series of nightly sorties into London from his estate.

Harker's horrifying experiences in Transylvania, the death of his wife's best friend at the hands of the Count in Whitby and the suffering which his own wife undergoes at Purfleet, lead him – together with his wife, three friends and a certain Dr Van Helsing, an authority on the vampire legends of Eastern Europe – to follow a succession of clues on a relentless quest to track down the Count and rid the world of him and his fellow vampires once and for all. Ultimately, the Count is killed by the traditional method of plunging a stake through his heart, in the manner now immortalised by horror movies, before he can wreak any further havoc on the world.

A simple resume of *Dracula* such as the above cannot possibly do the novel justice and it is suggested that the work itself is read by those who wish to taste the flavour of Stoker's work first-hand, but the brief details given will suffice here for the purposes of supporting investigations into its links with Purfleet.

Despite the success of *Dracula*, Stoker's work at the theatre still had to go on. In 1905 Irving's company was in Bradford for a provincial tour of Tennyson's *Becket*. Back at their hotel, the Midland, after the performance, Irving collapsed. Stoker was summoned, but the great actor – who, in 1895, had become the first actor to be knighted – had died by the time he got there.

Stoker sought solace in his work. The theatre company still needed to be run and there were books to write. He penned his memoirs of the actor in his *Personal Reminiscences of Henry Irving* (1906) and wrote the horror story, *Snowbound* (1908). He wrote romances, fairy tales, stories of the supernatural and some works of non-fiction, but none of his other works was ever to achieve the success of *Dracula*.

On 20th April 1912, at the age of 64, the dependable theatre manager and writer died. The cause of death was given as 'exhaustion', though some have tried to claim that he died of syphilis. He was cremated in London and left one son, Noel.

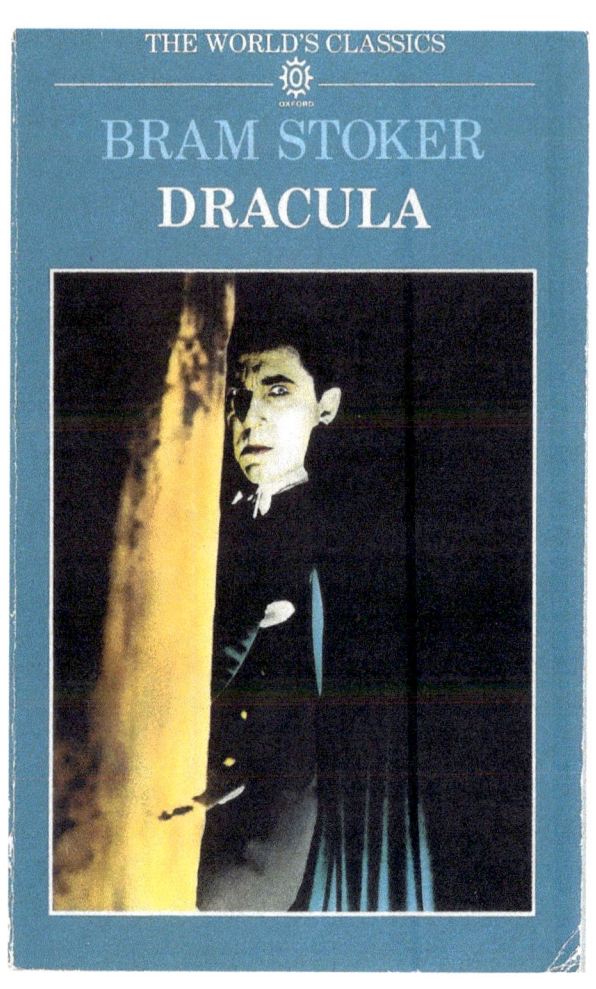

The actual copy of Dracula which was read by the author in 1990

II

BACKGROUND – VLAD DRACULA AND VAMPIRES

The horrors of *Dracula* may seem extreme, but there was a great deal of historical 'vampire' material for Stoker to draw upon. Listed sources that he is known to have used when researching *Dracula* include works on vampires, burial practices, ancient superstitions from Eastern Europe and North America, the relationship between the dead and the living, cannibalism, trances and sleepwalking, burial alive, Eastern European geography and peoples, the Devil, a history of Transylvania, giants, fairy tales, witchcraft, castles, blood-drinking, were-wolves and vampire bats, seafaring superstitions, meteorology, medicine, hypnotism and mesmerism, exorcism and the legal profession. Traces of all these subjects can be found in the novel.

A vampire is defined by the Oxford English Dictionary as follows: "A preternatural being of a malignant nature (in the original and usual form of the belief, a reanimated corpse), supposed to seek nourishment, or do harm, by sucking the blood of sleeping persons; a man or woman abnormally endowed with similar habits." Other sources add that it is supposedly the restless soul of a heretic, criminal or suicide that leaves its burial place at night, often in the form of a bat, to drink the blood of humans. It must return to its grave, or to a coffin filled with its native earth, by daybreak. Its victims become vampires after death. It is a mythical creature which possesses a dead body and the body's former owner's soul.

In Eastern Europe particularly, there were strong beliefs in vampires and there was even a vampire "epidemic" in Hungary in the 1720s and 1730s when the population became hysterical with fear about the creatures. Even before that, there were examples of vampire behaviour, with the infamous practices of the Countess Elizabeth Bathory who bathed in human blood to keep her youthful looks and the mass-murders by Gilles de Rais (or Retz), also known as 'Bluebeard'. But the individual on whom Stoker seems to have based much of his central character was a 15th-century Romanian tyrant, the Prince of Wallachia, Vlad Dracula (1431-1476).

Wallachia was a neighbouring province to Transylvania and Vlad ruled the land with an iron hand. He murdered countless enemies, including fellow Wallachian noblemen whom he saw as a threat to his position, and hundreds of civilians, particularly dishonest people and women (especially) who were lazy or immoral. He once treated all the poor and weak in the district to a slap-up meal in his palace and then set fire to it with them inside, the justification for this act being that he had removed all poverty and illness from his province at a stroke. Another infamous act of his was the nailing of turbans to the heads of some Turkish ambassadors (the Turks were Wallachia's enemies) when the ambassadors refused to remove their turbans because it was against their religion. He is said to have killed more than 100,000 people in total.

Vlad Dracula was evidently a cruel and violent man whose favourite method of execution was to impale his victims on a vertical wooden stake. This method of death was a slow and agonising one, as the weight of the individual was all that determined the speed with which death came. Because of this practice, Vlad gained the nickname of "Vlad the Impaler" and the wooden stake, as all *Dracula* followers know, later appeared in Stoker's novel as the method by which a vampire could be killed.

Other methods of killing vampires were drawn from Eastern European legends, which describe the vampire as a formidable creature. Living by night and sleeping by day, it can change its form (usually into a bat or a wolf), it can create a disguising mist around it at any time by which to effect an unseen escape and it is possessed of formidable strength. It can make itself small enough to slide through the narrow cracks under doors and around window frames and can see in the dark.

But it is not without its weaknesses. It cannot cross running water, except at the slack or the flood of the tide. It must sleep between sunrise and sunset – its most vulnerable time – as its power ceases at the coming of day. Even at night it may be warded off with crucifixes, garlic and the branch of the wild rose – but it can be killed only by having a stake driven through its heart and then by having its head cut off – only then will the soul of the person whose body it has taken over be freed. This is precisely the end that meets the vampire in Stoker's novel.

Stoker's *Dracula* was by no means the first work of fiction to tackle the subject of vampires. Lord Byron and others had written stories about vampires and there were even operas and plays about them, but Stoker's novel represented the culmination of vampire literature, becoming the classic gothic horror novel.

In Stoker's day, there was a good deal of interest in Wallachia, Transylvania and Moldavia, the three provinces which were later to unite into Romania, for several reasons.

Factual books about the area were beginning to appear and Transylvania's Queen Elizabeth of Wied was writing novels about her home country. A travelling exhibition on Eastern Europe visited London in the 1880s and there was much talk of the union of Wallachia and Moldavia into one country. Even Royalty was not immune from involvement – Queen Victoria's grand-daughter married into an Eastern European Royal family. Setting a story of ancient superstitions in modern-day London – the largest and most civilised city in the world at the time – was a masterstroke.

The significant thing was that *Dracula* was a "real" horror novel. Its readers were asked to believe that the action in it had really taken place – the vampire was not explained away at the end of the novel by some scientific means. London had really been under threat from a formidable opponent, whose operations had been based just a few miles down the Thames to the east, at the Essex marshland village of Purfleet.

III

THE PURFLEET CONNECTION

Stoker's associations with Irving's theatrical company and the acquaintances which he made with other leading figures in the worlds of art and literature through his position at the Lyceum ensured that he was an accepted part of London society, gaining invitations to many prestigious and lavish social events. It was the fashion of many leading society figures of the day to take a trip down the Thames from London to the little out-of-the-way Thameside village of Purfleet, where they would feast on the culinary delights of the "legendary" whitebait suppers prepared by Mr John George Wingrove, proprietor of the waterside *Royal Hotel*.

According to an 1872 guidebook, the *Royal Hotel* was built on the site of an earlier inn called the *Ship* and was "a favourite resort" of city men and their families which was famed for its whitebait and general cuisine. The opening of the London, Tilbury and Southend railway line in 1854 also attracted wealthy Londoners to what, up until then, had been (rather like Transylvania) a largely unknown and mysterious place, despite its proximity to the capital.

The *Royal Hotel* was also at one time known as the *Bricklayers' Arms*, because of its connection with the Bricklayers' Company of London which held extensive chalk quarries in the locality, and throughout the nineteenth century it was frequented by numerous celebrities and social lions. Rumour has it that Edward VII, when Prince of Wales, paid secret visits to it (hence the Royal dedication) and there is evidence that the Irish patriot Charles Stewart Parnell used to stay there when visiting his mistress, Katherine "Kitty" O'Shea, at the now-demolished Belhus mansion in nearby Aveley.

Purfleet c.1918, showing The Royal Hotel on the left

Leading theatrical figures with whom Stoker was personally acquainted are known to have visited the *Royal Hotel* and the book *Estuary*, by A K Astbury (Carnforth Press, 1980), quotes a reference of Stoker's to "the wonderful smoky beauty of a sunset over London, with its lurid lights and inky shadows and all the marvellous tints that come on foul clouds even as on foul water", which suggests that he himself had witnessed just such a sunset from somewhere on the lower Thames – surely Purfleet. There is also evidence that Stoker visited Gravesend, on the other side of the Thames, to receive a "splendid" silver-topped cane of black zebra wood, inscribed "Presented to Bram Stoker Esq by the crew of *U.S. Chicago* 1894"; the *U.S. Chicago* was a ship which was moored off the town at the time.

In addition, Stoker was a renowned walker – he spent much time in Scotland (particularly at Cruden Bay in Aberdeenshire) and in other parts of Britain exploring the countryside – and at Purfleet, too, there can be no doubt that he took time out to investigate the locality and familiarise himself with features of the natural landscape and individuals of the local community.

The ornamental gardens of the nearby "Botany" – later, in the years up to 1914, to be used as a location for the shooting of western and war films – would surely have been, as they were to countless other people, one of the obvious places to visit. Stoker's great nephew, Daniel Farson, records that the author's holidays were never "idle affairs" – "like Charles Dickens, he strode cheerfully through the country on long walking tours... with his photographic memory, he transformed the places he visited into locations for future stories. Not only could he conjure up atmosphere from musty books in the British Museum, but also he utilised every place he did visit, exploiting every detail. He did this at Boscastle [in Cornwall] ... Cruden Bay... and Whitby [where a great sailing ship, just like the Count's, was washed up on the shore a few years before *Dracula* was published]." Stoker's descriptions of London buildings in *Dracula* can also be traced to the originals that he must have visited. There is therefore no reason to think that he did not similarly utilise in the novel the Purfleet locations that he evidently encountered.

The development of Purfleet village was, historically-speaking, very late. A hamlet of West Thurrock, it was first recorded in 1285, though it had Knights Templar origins in the late 12th century. The community grew up on high ground, which has now been extensively quarried away, at the western end of the parish near the mouth (pur) of the river Mardyke (fleet) and over the next four hundred years houses began to appear on both sides of the main road from Grays to London. This pattern remained unchanged until the late 18th century.

Tourists at The Botany ornamental gardens c.1911, a popular 19th-century attraction

Purfleet's modern growth began in 1760, when the government of the day decided to build its dry storage gunpowder magazines at the mouth of the Mardyke, next to the Thames, where shipments could easily be loaded and unloaded and where powder was held at a suitable proximity to London to be quickly accessible yet at a safe enough distance if ever there should be any accidental explosions. The magazines cost £15,000 to erect and covered an area of 25 acres. Each of them could hold some 10,000 barrels of gunpowder and was 152 feet long by 52 feet wide, with walls that were five feet thick. There was copper sheathing on the doors and window openings and the walls were lined with wood. The roofs were supported by carefully designed brick arches. Powder was also later stored in two ships anchored in the Thames nearby – the *Conquestador* and the *Mermaid* – and although all British military stations were supplied with powder from the stores until circa 1950 (they proved to be particularly useful during the First World War), there were fortunately never any accidents at the development.

In 1769 a clocktower with distinctive archway was built and other administrative and military buildings were also provided at various times. The magazines finally closed in 1962 and in the 1970s all buildings on what became known as the Royal Ordnance development, except number 5 magazine, a barrel store, the Ordnance House Headquarters (destroyed by fire in 1972) and the clocktower, were demolished to make way for the Garrison housing estate.

No.5 Gunpowder Magazine – the sole such survivor on the Ordnance site; now Purfleet Heritage & Military Centre

The Garrison entrance c.1915, showing the clocktower in the background

Apart from the Ordnance grounds, the main buildings in the area on John Chapman and Peter André's famous 1777 map of Essex are High House and Stone House, though by 1791 the brewer, Samuel Whitbread, had taken on much of the land and had built both his own home, Purfleet House, and a chapel, a school, a schoolhouse dwelling and two rows of cottages in "The Dipping", an old chalk quarry, for the families of those whom he employed to operate his quarrying business (where perhaps, incidentally, was established the first railway in Essex in 1807). The chalk hereabouts is some 750 feet deep below the surface and, at one time, quarrying was so extensive that deposits were sent to America for cement making.

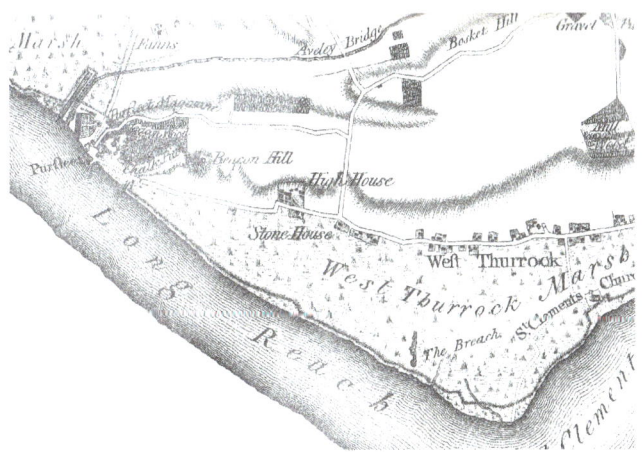

Purfleet as shown on John Chapman & Peter André's Map of Essex from 1777

The chapel was used by Whitbread as a meeting house for his family and workers – who were all required to attend – and was, at the time, the only place in Purfleet where Church of England services were held. Workers were summoned to prayer by an old bell hung on the branch of a tree, as there was no bell-tower in the structure. The waterside *Royal Hotel* was also once in Whitbread's ownership.

In the mid-19th century Purfleet became a popular resort, with, initially, wealthy 'city men' and society figures and later, when there were cheap-day rail fares from London, ordinary folk being attracted to the place. The railway network, of course, provided easy access to many other places of interest in the country which had hitherto been inaccessible in a day and eventually, because of this, interest amongst day trippers to Purfleet gradually began to decline.

In 1990 the principal feature of the village, if it can still be called that, was the dominating presence of the Thameside oil industries which took hold of the area after the Whitbread family's huge estates were sold at auction in 1920, after well over a hundred years in their private ownership. Now (2018), this industrial impact has decreased a little, but the amount of residential development has significantly increased. The M25 motorway and the Queen

Elizabeth II Bridge pass by to the east only a couple of miles away and a stream of Heavy Goods Vehicles thunders through the narrow streets around the area on a multitude of errands to and from the factories and facilities thereabouts. The Royal Opera House's "High House Production Park" has appeared in the village since the Millennium and the equally new Channel Tunnel rail route has required a new bridge through the area over London Road to the east of the village.

In the late-19th century, only the Thames Board Paper Mills and the Standard Oil company (now Esso) had industrial facilities at Purfleet. It is no longer a little out of the way place, an Essex marshland village popular with day-tripping Londoners, wishing to get away from it all. Stoker would not know the place if he were to return there now.

Purfleet Railway Station, c.1911

IV

THE *ROYAL HOTEL* AND THE PURFLEET FERRY

Some people think it strange that Stoker should have chosen a place like Purfleet – an unknown, insignificant and out-of-the-way place as it was then – as one of the principal locations for a gothic horror novel when, imaginative an author as he was, he could with less effort have used somewhere more atmospheric, like Dartmoor, for instance, to equal effect. But then Purfleet, with its gouged-out quarries and rolling sea mists, and with the unique capacity of being a place known to the literary set, yet unknown to the Victorian reader at large, could very easily have been conceived as a very real setting for such strange things as surreptitious vampire activities.

As mentioned earlier, *Dracula* was to be a real horror story and Londoners would believe the story more if it happened close to London. The fact is that Stoker knew the place and saw how its loneliness and remoteness could be used to great effect in the story of a murderous Count from far away Transylvania – Purfleet, too, relatively speaking, was a vaguely mysterious and faraway place.

Not everything has changed since Stoker's day, of course, and there are several Purfleet locations worthy of closer inspection with respect to the work of the author of *Dracula*.

The *Royal Hotel*, for example, is still there and although it is not specifically mentioned in *Dracula* the alleyway which passes beside it to the east does get a mention. When the Count's home at a place called *Carfax* is discovered by Jonathan Harker and his companions as they begin to close the net around him in their quest to destroy him, the alleyway beside the hotel, which at one time led to the Purfleet ferry, is used by the Count to escape to the river and across to Bermondsey. When he moves to England, the Count brings with him 50 boxes of "hallowed" earth, within any one of which he will be safe throughout the hours of daylight and has these delivered initially to *Carfax* in one consignment. Bit by bit, however, he moves them out to other areas around London to provide himself with bases where he can stay so that he does not have to return to Purfleet all the time. He is still in the process of doing this when Harker and his friends discover 29 of the boxes at *Carfax*. When the Count finds that these boxes have been destroyed, he crosses the Thames to Bermondsey to check on others which he has hidden in a property there and Harker's wife,

Mina, who is temporarily staying at Dr John Seward's neighbouring lunatic asylum (as a guest, not a patient), witnesses his departure from Purfleet down the accessway next to the *Royal Hotel* which leads to the ferry.

The pathway next to The Royal Hotel that once led to Purfleet ferry

Thurrock historian, F Z Claro, writing in 1966, recorded that Purfleet ferry, which operated from the *Royal Hotel* across to the *Long Reach Tavern* on Dartford marshes was mentioned frequently in early records (at least four hundred previously) and crossed to "within living memory" at that time. It was, he said, only a few years earlier that the waterman's stairs leading up to the *Long Reach Tavern* on the Kent side were demolished. The *Tavern* itself has also now disappeared, though the name was at one time (including in the 1990s) commemorated in the *Royal Hotel's* south-facing "Long Reach Bar" – the "Long Reach" is the name for that part of the Thames which extends from Crayfordness to Greenhithe and on which are situated the towns of Purfleet and West Thurrock. The Essex equivalent of these steps, the "King's Stairs", which were built to allow watermen and villagers using the ferry to bypass the nearby Ordnance grounds on which the gunpowder magazines stood, thus obviating the need to trespass on those grounds, have also been demolished since Claro's report.

The Purfleet ferry, which must not be confused with several similar ventures which have operated in this area of the Thames, was mentioned by Philip Morant in his *The History & Antiquities of the County of Essex* in 1768, eight years after the powder magazines were established. The inference in Claro's (and other) reports is that the ferry stopped running in the late 19th century, round about the time of Stoker's visits, but even if the author himself did not use it he could easily have heard tales about the ferry from old residents or guests of the hotel who had either used it themselves or had seen it in use.

Thus, the first piece of Purfleet fact (the river crossing) became incorporated into *Dracula* fiction. But apart from the *Royal Hotel* and the alleyway to the ferry, there are several other clues to be found in *Dracula* as to the real-life identity of some of the features mentioned in the novel. By far and away the most important of these is the Count's Purfleet home – *Carfax* – the subject of the most important chapter of this book.

V

CARFAX

When, in *Dracula*, the estate agent's representative, Jonathan Harker, is giving the Count details of the property that he has found for him, a detailed description of the building and its environs is provided:

"At Purfleet, on a by-road, I came across just such a place as seemed to be required, and where was displayed a dilapidated notice that the place was for sale. It is surrounded by a high wall, of ancient structure, built of heavy stones, and has not been repaired for a large number of years. The closed gates were of heavy old oak and iron, all eaten with rust.

"The estate is called 'Carfax', no doubt a corruption of the old 'Quatre Fois', as the house is four-sided, agreeing with the cardinal points of the compass. It contains in all some 20 acres, quite surrounded by the solid stone wall above mentioned. There are many trees on it, which make it in places gloomy, and there is a deep, dark-looking pond or small lake, evidently fed by some springs, as the water is clear and flows away in a fair-sized stream. The house is very large and of all periods back, I should say, to medieval times, for one part is of stone immensely thick, with only a few windows high up and heavily barred with iron. It looks like part of a keep and is close to an old chapel or church. The house has been added to, but in a very straggling way, and I can only guess at the amount of ground it covers, which must be very great. There are but few houses close at hand, one being a very large house only recently added to and formed into a private lunatic asylum. It is not, however, visible from the grounds."

This could almost be Stoker himself relating to his literary friends an account of how he went for a walk around Purfleet and came across a distinctive building which he later resurrected for use in his novel, just as he had resurrected local features of other towns and villages for use in other novels. But was it a real building and, if so, which building was it?

The elaborate description of *Carfax* in *Dracula* can be considered detailed enough to enable the recognition of the house on which it is based, if such a house ever existed. Today, though, there is no building of that description in the village. However, according to David Weaver, in his 1985 book, *Essex Tales*, which was broadcast in a series of programmes on Essex Radio during that year, there were at least two places carrying the name of *Carfax* in Purfleet, neither of which matched Stoker's description.

The name *Carfax* is unusual, so it seems quite incredible that there could be more than one place bearing it in the village. Funnily enough, Stoker refers later in the novel to the village of Carfax in Sussex – to where an important telegram is accidentally and crucially misdirected – so perhaps this was the only Carfax with which he, like most other people, had been familiar until his fateful trip to Purfleet.

Even so, up until early summer 1990, there was indeed one *Carfax*, at least, to be found in London Road, Purfleet, something like half a mile to the east of Purfleet station. A large red-brick detached two-storey house with white window frames, green paintwork and a green front door, it looked very little like the building described in such graphic detail above and nothing at all like one which might be expected to house the sinister lair of an evil and bloodthirsty "Prince of Darkness". Significantly, this building was erected in the 1890s – when Stoker would be most likely to have been in Purfleet for one of the many events which were held at the *Royal Hotel* – and, equally significantly, it was completed in 1897, the very year that *Dracula* was published. It is quite conceivable that, on one of his walks around the locality Stoker had seen the house being built, had liked the sound of the name and had incorporated it into the horror novel that he was planning at that time. The building was certainly known as *Carfax* throughout its life.

The last owners of this Purfleet building experienced many problems from prospective vampire hunters because of the name's associations with Count Dracula and it was largely this which made them move out. Shortly before leaving the property in 1990, however, one of the owners, Lilla E. Dixson, left the author this record of her time there:

> "We have suffered a lot because of the association. In fact, up to ten years ago [i.e. *c.*1980], every time the BBC put out a *Dracula* programme we had stones through our windows; filth through our letterbox; damage all-round the place. The final straw being when I opened my door one evening to about a score of youths armed with stakes, who tried to hurl them at me. I got the door shut in time."

Regrettably, almost as soon as those last owners had left (so, around May/June 1990), the building was demolished. For a time, the fenced-off site remained, the green gate, with the word *Carfax* painted on it in dripping black letters, hanging off its hinges in the undergrowth.

The land on which the building stood was originally owned by the Thames Board Mills but later became the property of Esso Petroleum, along with a site alongside it on which once stood the four 1890s-built "High House Cottages".

Carfax, photographed by the author in February 1990

Research in the 1970s by an American writer and members of the Thurrock Local History Society has, however, shown that it is not this nor any other *Carfax* on which Stoker's building is based. When delving into the archives, one can see almost immediately from surviving reports and photographs that the description above fits not *Carfax*, but Samuel

Whitbread's old mansion in The Dipping (or "Dipping Hollow") – Purfleet House.

The sale catalogue of the Whitbread estate when put to auction in 1920, gives perhaps the most detailed description of the appearance of the two properties and therefore provides the best guide on which to base any attempted comparisons:

"Lot 24A: The freehold property *Carfax* situated on the north side of High Road about half a mile from Purfleet Station, consisting of a red brick and tiled modern residence approached from the road along an excellent gravelled path and fronted by a large lawn and having neatly kept flower borders and kitchen gardens.

"The residence, which is comfortably planned, contains the following accommodation:-

"On the upper floor – four bedrooms, bathroom, lavatory and WC

"On the ground floor – small inner hall, drawing and dining rooms, small morning room, kitchen, scullery, lavatory and WC.

"There is an addition, comprising washhouse with copper, two sinks and coal cellar.

"Hot and cold water services and gas.

"Let on lease to the Thames Paper

Company for 72 years from 25th December 1900 at a ground rent of £15 per annum.
"The tithes have been apportioned by the auctioneers for the purposes of this sale as under:-

"Parish of West Thurrock – Vicarial 1s; value for 1920 1s 1d.
"Parish of West Thurrock – Impropriate 2s 7d; value for 1920 2s 10d."

[According to the *Grays & Thurrock Gazette*, the property sold for £250.]

Purfleet, from a 19th-century illustration

"Lot 40: The residence known as *Purfleet House* situated in the village of Purfleet and within a few minutes' walk of the railway station. The house, which has balconies to the first and second floors, stands well back from the High Road, and is fronted by a well-laid and shrub-bordered lawn. It is substantially constructed of brick, with tiled roof; the principal rooms face south and are old-fashioned in design.

"The accommodation is as follows:-

"On the upper floor – five bedrooms, housemaid's sink, WC

"On the first floor – nine bed and dressing rooms (some fitted with spacious wardrobe cupboards); bathroom; WC; housemaid's sink; WC [sic]; six other bedrooms reached by separate staircase

"On the ground floor – portico entrance; hall; dining room (22' by 20'); drawing room (26' by 23'), with large bay and casement windows opening on to lawn; morning room; WC

"The domestic offices consist of servants' hall, housemaid's room with extensive cupboards, pantry and strong room; still room, large paved kitchen and store adjoining. There are large cellars; heating room and dairy.

"The house is fitted with hot and cold water services, and gas is laid on.

"The outbuildings consist of knife and boot houses, coal and wood lodges, boiling house, bake house, game larder and two WCs.

"The pleasure garden adjoins the residence to the west, and is disposed in neatly arranged flower beds, and contains some fine ornamental trees.

"To the north east of the residence, and flanked by a top terrace walk with picturesque summerhouse, is a fine old sunken garden under full cultivation and plentifully stocked with mixed fruit trees; also, a capital brick and slated cottage, as well as the brick and slated church, with the adjoining land and schoolroom.

"The church, schoolroom and land therewith are sold subject to the right of the Vicar of West Thurrock to have the use and enjoyment thereof, together with a right of access to such premises along the roadway for all purposes in connection with such church, schoolroom and land. The right of removing the existing church and buildings within three calendar months of the consecration of the new church is reserved to the Vicar.

"The total area of this lot is 5 acres 2 rods

20 perches or thereabouts. [Together
with the 14 acres of Lot 2, The Dipping,
adjoining the railway sidings at Purfleet
station and withdrawn at £5000, this
would have made almost exactly the 20
acres of the *Carfax* in Stoker's novel,
all of which was enclosed by the "high
surrounding wall".]

"And, with the exception of the cottage,
which is let to Mr Howe at 4s 6d per week,
also subject to the provision in regard
to the church and schoolroom before
mentioned, vacant possession will be given
upon completion.

"The vendor reserves the right to hold
an auction on the premises prior to
completion.

"Included with this lot will be a Right of
Way over the roadway coloured brown on
the plan [a fenced-off curving track still
there in 1990 which led down to the old
chapel, the school and the schoolhouse
cottage in the chalk quarry behind Church
Hollow, but which is now no longer
accessible] in common with the vendor and
the purchasers of such other lots as abut
thereon so far as it may benefit this lot.

"The purchaser will be required to erect a
fence along the south eastern boundary, as
shown by the dotted line between the point

L and the point M [on the above-mentioned plan], dividing this lot from lot 41.

"The tithes have been apportioned by the Auctioneers for the purposes of this sale as under:-

"Parish of West Thurrock: Vicarial 9s 3d; value for 1920, 10s 1d.

" Ditto [sic] : Impropriate 2s 9d; value for 1920, 3s 0d."

The sale of the whole estate of 342 acres (in 57 lots), which stretched almost to Stonehouse corner, West Thurrock, raised something like £124,000.

There were, of course, some similarities between all three properties in question: Stoker's *Carfax* was "at Purfleet, on a by-road" – so had been both the real *Carfax* and Purfleet House; his was large and square, four-sided "agreeing with the cardinal points of the compass" – so were they. But there were also certain obvious similarities between Stoker's *Carfax* and Purfleet House which were not shared by the real *Carfax*.

Stoker's *Carfax*, for example, like Purfleet House, had many trees around it – it is described rather pictorially in the novel by the character of Dr Van Helsing as being a "walled park" – whilst the real *Carfax* did not. The first two had few houses in their immediate vicinity (Purfleet House was in an area on its own in a vast quarry), whilst the real *Carfax* had the four High House Cottages built right next to it, which had been erected seven years before it had been constructed and which must therefore have been there throughout most of its early life and which were certainly there at the time when Stoker was most likely to have seen it. Stoker's *Carfax* was surrounded by a high wall (high enough for Dr Seward to require a ladder to negotiate it when pursuing Renfield, his escaping mental patient), as was Purfleet House – but there was simply a low wooden fence at the real *Carfax*. Similarly, Stoker's building had heavy old oak and iron gates, as did Whitbread's mansion, rather than just one of the modest standard garden variety. And, perhaps most significantly, Stoker's *Carfax* and Purfleet House both had an "old chapel or church" nearby (Whitbread's 1791 chapel would certainly have been old when Stoker saw it in the 1890s), whilst the real *Carfax* had none.

It is apparent, then, that the only thing that Stoker used from the real *Carfax* for his fictional one was the name. Everything else was based on Purfleet House.

Parts of the high wall surrounding Purfleet House are still there, even though the mansion itself was demolished in 1951. The *Grays & Thurrock Gazette* of 21st April that year, under the headline *Beer Magnate's Mansion Demolished*, contained a photo of Purfleet House being knocked down – it was just visible behind the trees. The house had 26 rooms – certainly large enough to fit Stoker's *Carfax* description. The house was, in fact, so big that "troops of the Kaiser" were "held prisoners of war in the old mansion", which "caused one of the biggest stirs Purfleet has ever known". Interestingly, unlike the passing of Purfleet House almost 40 years earlier, the demise of *Carfax* in 1990 was not considered significant enough to be afforded generous media coverage.

The "old chapel or church", with its "iron-bound oak door", survived intact into the 1990s, though it looked very tatty, with ivy clinging to the north side and almost completely smothering its little single-storey extension. Even in *Dracula* (therefore circa 1897) it is described as a "partially ruined building". The structure, though originally white, was in 1990 very black and grimy, thanks to the ill-treatment of time and neglect. The school and schoolhouse cottage were also still there, though both were in as dilapidated a condition as the chapel and were almost entirely hidden by unkempt undergrowth.

Since then the whole site has been fenced off and is now inaccessible, with a notice announcing that there are "dangerous buildings" on the site. The chapel has become increasingly derelict but can be glimpsed through the fencing and undergrowth from the relatively new Caspian Way. It is impossible to see the school or the schoolhouse from the public road. Aerial views from available Internet-mapping services suggest that they are still there but crumbling. It can surely be only a matter of time before all three buildings are demolished and the part of the quarry that they occupied is redeveloped for housing.

The "old chapel or church", photographed by the author in 1990

VI

DR SEWARD'S ASYLUM

So much for Count Dracula's abode, but what of the asylum which stood next it? Was there ever such an establishment adjacent to the real *Carfax,* or did this, too, have more in common with Purfleet House, if, indeed, it ever existed at all?

There are, in fact, several candidates for the model for the asylum.

In the early years of the 20th century and the last years of the 19th – and certainly in 1897, when *Dracula* was published – there was a hospital building immediately to the west of the *Royal Hotel,* which remained there until at least the start of the Second World War. It, along with several other buildings nearby, was later demolished and never subsequently replaced. This hospital occupied part of what is now the open 'green' between the *Royal Hotel* and the Garrison housing estate. The second edition OS map of 1897 shows a hospital on the edge of the river, just west of the *Royal Hotel* and between it and the powder magazines, but there is no reference to it being an asylum.

There was also once another hospital hereabouts on the Kent side of the Thames. Old residents remember smallpox cases being ferried down from London for treatment at the establishment, which, like the *Long Reach Tavern*, stood on the Dartford Marshes. Stoker may well have seen one of these boats in operation when visiting Purfleet and such a sight could easily have stirred in him horrifying memories of his own sickly and bedridden childhood.

The river itself also played host to at least one other unusual kind of institution at a time when Stoker would have been at Purfleet, though this, too, was not quite in the realms of a lunatic asylum. This was the Training Ship *Cornwall*, which was moored off Purfleet and was designed as a kind of reform school for friendless and uncared-for boys. A similar experiment had been established in Liverpool in 1859 by Sir George Henry Chambers and the venture there had been so successful that Chambers was prompted to set up a second ship a Purfleet. Although the *Cornwall*, under the captaincy, in the early- to mid-1890s, of one Arthur Morrell, was later replaced by the *HMS Wellesley* (which was renamed the *Cornwall* for the purposes of continuity), the venture still managed to last for over 80 years. It catered for some 200-250 boys at a time and its anchorage in the Thames, just off the *Royal Hotel*, would have put it in a prominent position for a sighting by river travellers from

London and diners at the waterside hotel. A grave of some of the ship's company can be seen in the churchyard of St Clement's church, West Thurrock.

Back on land, there was also once some kind of asylum, too, some miles east of Purfleet, in Meeson's Lane, West Thurrock, but this seems too remote from the area to be the one which Stoker saw.

Stoker, remember, says of the asylum in his description of the *Carfax* estate:

"There are but few houses close at hand [i.e. close to *Carfax*], one being a very large house only recently added to and formed into a private lunatic asylum. It is not, however, visible from the grounds."

The only properties near to the "real" London Road *Carfax* were the four High House Cottages, which, by comparison, were immediately adjacent to it, were not of substantial size and could easily be seen from the grounds.

Purfleet House, on the other hand, had a high wall surrounding it, which would most certainly have obscured the view of any surrounding property. So, what was near Purfleet House?

To the north were (and still are, to a degree) the old chapel, the school and the schoolhouse cottage. To the east, the two rows of workers' cottages built by Whitbread could hardly be considered big enough, by any stretch of the imagination, to be mistaken for the expected asylum, whilst to the south the *Royal Hotel* was simply a place where the needs of centuries of famished and thirsty travellers and diners had been, and were still being, catered for. The current church of St Stephen and the nearby vicarage were not built until c.1923, so Stoker could not possibly have seen these (he died in 1912, remember).

Incidentally, St Stephen's, intended to be a 'temporary' ecclesiastical home when erected, was retained as a church because there was never sufficient money available to build the dreamed-of new one. According to a 1951 newspaper report: "Since the days of the planned new church, people in Purfleet have got disheartened and lost interest. Fewer people are going to church – so we shall continue to use the 'temporary building'."

That leaves the west, then – and curiously enough it was the western boundary of the site around which ran (and still in part does run) the view-obscuring "high surrounding wall".

Over the London Road to the west of the old site of Purfleet House stands the residential development of the Garrison housing estate. In Stoker's day the Royal Ordnance grounds would have had an exclusively military purpose here. The asylum in the novel is referred to as "recently added to" and additions were being made to the sprawling Garrison development all the time. This military estate, with its powder storehouses and barracks, was certainly an institution of a kind.

Curiously, the records of the Esso Petroleum company at Purfleet refer to there having once been an asylum in the vicinity and, most significantly, "an archway is still standing which was the entrance to the asylum". The only archway in the area today is to be found on the Garrison housing estate – that of the clocktower which was once a part of the huge government development – and, despite its size, this cannot be seen from Dipping Hollow.

Although it is reasonable to assume that a hospital existed on the site, in case of accident, there is no proof that it has ever been used as an asylum. Despite this, three points taken from the novel in connection with the geographical relation of the asylum to *Carfax* (Purfleet House, for our purposes) are of note.

Firstly, Dr Seward, when standing at what he refers to on at least two occasions as the asylum "gateway" one evening early in September, is awoken from his thoughts by the sounds of Renfield (the mental patient) yelling in his room and recalls: "It was a shock to me to turn from the wonderful smoky beauty of a sunset over London... and to realise all the grim sternness of my own stone cold building, with its wealth of breathing misery, and my own desolate heart to endure it all". Since the sun always sets in the west and the view in front of him is not obscured by any other structure, it is reasonable to assume that *Carfax* stands behind him and therefore to the east of the asylum.

Secondly, in support of this supposition, when Count Dracula later attacks Mina at the asylum, one of her husband's companions, Quincey Morris, tells Dr Van Helsing: "I saw a bat rise from Renfield's window, and flap westward... I expected to see him in some shape go back to *Carfax*; but he evidently sought some other lair". This, too, implies that *Carfax* stands to the east of the asylum in the novel – just as Purfleet House stood to the east of the military institution.

Thirdly, as the men leave *Carfax* in pursuit of the Count after they have destroyed the 29 safe-haven "earthboxes" which have not yet been removed from there and head towards Purfleet station for a trip into Fenchurch Street, they must look back to the asylum to see Mina waving 'goodbye' to them. The station is to the east of where Purfleet House stood, so the men would be travelling eastwards to get to it. Looking back to the asylum from *Carfax* on their way to the train again implies that the asylum stands to the west of *Carfax*, just as the powder magazines and military establishment stood to the west of Purfleet House.

It therefore seems certain from the above that the asylum in the novel was based on Purfleet's military institution.

The clocktower of the Royal Ordnance development;this may have been the model for the asylum gateway in Dracula

VII

CHARACTERS AND VAMPIRES

There are, then, enough geographical similarities between the places mentioned in *Dracula* and their corresponding real-life Purfleet locations to say that one was based in part on the other. Stoker was in Purfleet in the 1890s and had a chance to look around the place and absorb details of its layout and features – that is undeniable. But what of the characters? Were any of those based on inhabitants of the village?

Unlike the buildings of a place, which are often recorded for posterity in documents and maps, its people are not always so well identified. Only those famous enough to have influenced the area are usually described in any detail. Some get into photographs as "candids" if they are lucky enough to be in the right place at the right time, but most are known only to their immediate families and their contemporary neighbours and friends. The evidence with which to compare Stoker's characters and the people whom he might have met on one of his outings to the *Royal Hotel* is therefore rather sketchy, to say the least.

Unfortunately, few of Stoker's characters are described in sufficient detail to be able to attempt a comparison between them and any real-life personality who may once have existed. Jonathan Harker, in the diaries which he kept at Castle Dracula, describes the principal character, the Count, as "a tall old man, clean-shaven save for a long, white moustache, and clad in black from head to foot without a single speck of colour about him anywhere... His face was a strong – a very strong – acquiline, with high bridge of the thin nose and peculiarly arched nostrils; with lofty domed forehead, and hair growing scantily round the temples, but profusely elsewhere. His eyebrows were very massive, almost meeting over the nose, and with bushy hair that seemed to curl in its own profusion. The mouth, so far as I could see it under the heavy moustache, was fixed and rather cruel-looking, with peculiarly sharp white teeth; these protruded over the lips, whose remarkable ruddiness showed astonishing vitality in a man of his years. For the rest, his ears were pale and at the tops extremely pointed; the chin was broad and strong, and the cheeks firm though thin. The general effect was one of extraordinary pallor... his hands were rather coarse – broad, with squat fingers... the nails were long and fine, and cut to a sharp point." (Note that this description bears little similarity to most of the classic cinematic depictions of the Count, where Dracula is often presented as a comparatively younger man, with slicked-back black hair and no drooping moustache.)

Later, in London, Harker's wife, Mina, sees the Count for the first time: "his face was not a good face; it was hard, and cruel... he looked so fierce and nasty".

Curiously, the description of Count Dracula above bears some comparison with Stoker's mentor, Sir Henry Irving, particularly when in costume during some of his more sinister performances. More importantly, it also has similarities with a well-known picture of Vlad Dracula (the so-called "Lubeck print"), with his drooping moustache and hard face, which Stoker is likely to have seen in the 1880s exhibition in London which presented details about the Wallachian tyrant to the Victorian public for probably the first time.

Other pictures of Vlad, such as early woodcuts and the equally famous "Innsbruck portrait", would seem to bear this out. On a different tack, it also calls to mind a description of Stoker's of his one-time idol, the poet Walt Whitman, with his "great shaggy masses of grey white hair" and thick white moustache.

The other "bad" character in the novel – Renfield, the principal patient in Dr John Seward's lunatic asylum – has some description ("sanguine temperament; great physical strength; morbidly excitable; periods of gloom ending in some fixed idea which I cannot make out"), but all the other leading characters, whom we read about through each other's journals, are described sparingly, with just enough details given about their natures to make them credible and almost nothing given about their appearances. Jonathan Harker is "a good specimen of manhood" and a "quiet, business-like gentleman". Arthur Holmwood (Lord Godalming) is a "tall, handsome, curly-haired man". Dr Seward is "handsome, well off, and of good birth... clever... resolute... imperturbable". Quincey Morris is an American and a "great-hearted, true gentleman", possibly based on one of Stoker's American acquaintances. Mina and Lucy are typical "heroine"-like pretty girls, who bring out the chivalry in all the male characters around them. Lucy even receives three proposals of marriage in one day.

Some critics have suggested that Mina is based on Henry Irving's leading lady, Ellen Terry, at which juncture it is interesting to note both that Terry spent some time of her own in a lunatic asylum studying patients during research for her role as Ophelia in Shakespeare's *Hamlet* and that Lucy compares herself to Ophelia when lying ill in bed, garlanded with vampire-repelling flowers and garlic. Terry, herself, even gets a complimentary passing name credit later in the novel. (She also has another Essex connection in that there is a commemorative plaque to her in the parish church at Little Easton, near Dunmow, which she visited several times).

It is also worth noting, if only because the name is so unusual, that the wife of one of the leading lights of the Golden Dawn Society, Samuel Liddell Mathers, was also called Mina. Interestingly, the Golden Dawn Society had a member who was described in society documentation as being an "old man, with thin neck, and long grey hair, he has acquiline nose" [sic] – there are shades of the Count here!

As for the character of Abraham Van Helsing, he is a typical professor, though it is highly likely that he was based on one of Stoker's London acquaintances, Dr Arminius Vambery, who also gets a name credit in the novel as being the person from whom the professor gets much of his information about the identification and destruction of vampires ("my friend Arminius"). Van Helsing "knows what he is talking about better than anyone else… is a philosopher and a metaphysician, and one of the most advanced scientists of his day… with an iron nerve, a temper of the ice brook, an indomitable resolution, self-command and toleration exalted from virtues to blessings, and the kindest and truest heart that beats". Furthermore, he is "a man of medium height, strongly built, with his shoulders set back over a broad, deep chest... the poise of the head strikes one at once as indicative of thought and power".

Stoker repeatedly acknowledges his own indebtedness to the Hungarian scholar, Vambery, on whom this description could have been based, as the main source for the specific connection which he has made of Dracula to vampirism. In his capacity as a University lecturer, Vambery was familiar with the history of Moldavia and Wallachia and was also aware of the fact that in Hungarian folklore and history Dracula was consistently held to be an arch villain and a clever ruler and that Hungarian vampire stories often associated the word "Dracul" with acts of vampirism. In 1886 an article identifying this latter point was published and must have been seen by both Vambery and Stoker.

As for Van Helsing's Christian name, "Abraham" is, of course, Stoker's own real first name and one theory goes so far as to suggest that the character of the professor was based, not on Vambery, but on Stoker himself.

Talking of names, a Joseph Harker and his father, William, were scene painters for Irving at the Lyceum and it could be that Jonathan's surname in the novel is taken from these. Alternatively, the policeman who witnessed a celebrated domestic dispute in London in 1887, in which vampirism allegedly took place and with which Stoker was apparently familiar, was called John Harker.

But any or all these characters could have been based in varying degrees on Stoker's theatrical friends or acquaintances, ex-colleagues from his earlier Civil Service life or inhabitants of Purfleet village. Without photographic evidence of all his associates and with such limited descriptions to go on, no firm conclusions can be drawn. The character of Count Dracula could have been based on Henry Irving (either the actor himself or one of his many characters) or on Vlad Dracula – physiological similarities exist for both. It could even be Mr Wingrove from the *Royal Hotel*, or an anonymous, cantankerous old villager who frequented his establishment, or, come to that, one of any number of the establishments which Stoker must have visited on his travels. Equally, it could be totally fictional, the product of a vivid imagination, borne of fear and of illness and suffering developed during a sickly childhood in Ireland.

The identities of the models for the characters of Dracula will, unlike the locations, probably therefore always remain a mystery.

VIII

PURFLEET AND THE SUPERNATURAL

All that remains now is to consider whether Purfleet was chosen as the location for *Dracula* because of any supernatural or ghostly associations. Stoker's own interest in this subject could have been furthered through his alleged connections with the notorious Golden Dawn Society and it could be that he saw in the recently-visited Purfleet a supernatural potential which matched that of his impending novel.

Unlike other villages in Essex, such as Canewdon, which is surrounded by legends and talcs of witchcraft and dcvilry, Purflcct does not seem to have any such folklore. It does not warrant a mention in any major guide to ghostly or supernatural activity in the county.

Other places that Stoker visited do have their "supernatural" attractions. Boscastle in Cornwall has its "Museum of Magic and Witchcraft", and Whitby, where Dracula's ship comes ashore, even has a "Dracula Experience" to complement the female ghost which reportedly frequents its abbey's grounds. Purfleet, lost in Thameside industry, has no such attraction.

Vampirism may seem to be a thing of the past, but there have surprisingly been some relatively recent examples in this country of vampire cases, notably in 1970 at Highgate cemetery in London. Nothing like this is recorded to have happened in Purfleet.

Other Essex places are also mentioned in *Dracula* (mostly because they are relevant to the plot), but the supernatural reputations of these places are equally limited. Harwich is referred to in passing by the Count when he asks Jonathan Harker about the legal proceedings regarding shipping goods from Transylvania to an English port. Presumably, Stoker knew Whitby better than the Essex town and opted for this as the actual destination.

Closer to London, Van Helsing takes rooms at the "Great Eastern Hotel" on Liverpool Street station, opened in 1884 and still there today as the "Andaz Hyatt", despite the passage of years and following a considerable facelift in the late 1980s/early 1990s. Liverpool Street station would, of course, have been the ideal starting point for a trip to Purfleet. On separate occasions, Van Helsing also meets Dr Seward at the station when arriving from his native Holland, presumably having first travelled by ship to the then bustling passenger transport terminal at Tilbury, and is then met by the doctor at Purfleet station where he arrives by train from London.

The other Essex-facing mainline station, Fenchurch Street, also provides a starting point from the capital for Purfleet. Dr Seward records in his diary: "...we took the Underground to Fenchurch Street, after I had sent a wire to my housekeeper to have a sitting-room and bedroom prepared at once [at the asylum] for Mrs Harker". Jonathan Harker, too, uses the London to Purfleet railway line.

The East London areas of Bethnal Green, Mile End and Poplar are also mentioned, either as the addresses of the carters who remove some of the Count's "earthboxes" from *Carfax* or as the locations of the places to where the boxes are delivered, but this must simply be to add credibility and atmosphere to the story, rather than for any specific purpose of intimating supernatural associations with these places.

Stoker did use *The Book of Were-Wolves*, by Essex-based parson, Sabine Baring-Gould, who held the living at East Mersea in the 1870s and 1880s, as a source document – but there is no mention of Purfleet in that.

Purfleet's supernatural history is therefore either very poorly documented, or non-existent. The latter would seem the more likely.

IX

CONCLUSIONS

In line with the foregoing, it is fair to say, then, that the following conclusions can be drawn from an analysis of the fact and fiction of Purfleet and *Dracula*:

1. Stoker's model for *Carfax* was Purfleet House. The size, design, location and nature of this latter building fit almost exactly the description of the estate in the novel, except perhaps the water running through the grounds (though this could have been taken from the nearby Mardyke river), and allowing, of course, for an acceptable degree of artistic licence.

2. The name, "Carfax", was taken from a building barely a mile or so up the road which was being erected at the time that Stoker was researching his novel, and which was seen by him during a perambulation of the area on one of his visits to Purfleet.

3. The lunatic asylum was based, in location and appearance terms at least, on the Royal Ordnance development which was built around the government's dry storage gunpowder magazines. This was an institution of a kind and the archway to it still exists, as the files of Esso Petroleum rather curiously record that the archway to the asylum does. It was therefore from here or hereabouts that Jonathan Harker's wife, Mina, had seen the fleeing Count make his escape to the Purfleet ferry along the alleyway beside the *Royal Hotel.*

4. The characters and names in the novel cannot be easily pinned down to individuals of the locality.

5. Purfleet has no known supernatural history that could have inspired Bram Stoker to base the novel there, but it would have been both more atmospheric and remote in the 1890s (and thus more suitable for a horror story) than the 21st-century visitor finds it today.

~

We are left, then, with some fact and some fiction – a novel worth reading and a place worth visiting, if only to enable comparison between the two for yourself...

BIBLIOGRAPHY

Auction Particulars for the Whitbread Estate (Daniel Watney and Sons, 1920)

Chapman & André's Map of Essex (1777)

Dracula [biography of Vlad Dracula], Radu Florescu and Raymond T McNally (Robert Hale & Co., 1973)

Dracula, Bram Stoker (Oxford University Press, 1987) (originally 1897)

Essex Countryside, Vol.27, No.273, pp.36-38 (October 1979)

Essex Tales, David Weaver (Ian Henry Publications, 1985)

Estuary, A K Astbury (Carnforth Press, London, 1980)

Purfleet, I G Sparkes (Essex County Libraries, 1963)

The Bram Stoker Bedside Companion, Edited by Charles Osborne (Victor Gollancz Ltd, 1973)

The Dracula Centenary Book, Peter Haining (Souvenir Press, 1987)

The Golden Dawn Companion, R A Gilbert (The Aquarian Press, 1986)

The History & Antiquities of the County of Essex, Philip Morant (T. Osborne, 1768)

The Man Who Wrote 'Dracula', Daniel Farson (Michael Joseph, 1975)

The Origins of Dracula, Clive Leatherdale (William Kimber & Co., 1987)

Thurrock Gazette, (26.06.1920 and 21.04.1951)

Thurrock Local History Society Journal Vol. 8 (1963)

Various historical maps and documents at the Essex Record Office

Victoria County History Vol. 8 (Essex County Libraries, 1983)

ACKNOWLEDGEMENTS

A. Asplin/*Purfleet Baptist Church*

B.G. Holloway/*Esso Petroleum*

Chris Harrold/*Thurrock Local History Society*

Helena Gibbons

John Carswell

Lilla E. Dixson

N.B. Redman/*Whitbread & Co. Plc*

Paul Shelley/*Thurrock Borough Council*

Staff *at the Essex Record Office*

www.ingramcontent.com/pod-product-compliance
Lightning Source LLC
Chambersburg PA
CBHW041755180626
46815CB00018B/316